THE
Wild Swans
AN ADVENTURE IN SIX PARTS

Retold by **KEN SETTERINGTON**

Art by **NELLY & ERNST HOFER**

TUNDRA BOOKS

Text copyright © 2003 by Ken Setterington
Illustrations copyright © 2003 by Nelly and Ernst Hofer

Published in Canada by Tundra Books,
481 University Avenue, Toronto, Ontario M5G 2E9

Published in the United States by Tundra Books of Northern New York,
P.O. Box 1030, Plattsburgh, New York 12901

Library of Congress Control Number: 2003100907

National Library of Canada Cataloguing in Publication

Setterington, Ken
      The wild swans / retold by Ken Setterington ; art by Nelly and Ernst Hofer.
ISBN 0-88776-615-3

I. Hofer, Nelly II. Hofer, Ernst, 1961- III. Title.

PS8587.E835W54 2003   jC813'.6   C2003-900695-6
PZ7

We acknowledge the financial support of the Government of Canada through the Book
Publishing Industry Development Program and that of the Government of Ontario
through the Ontario Media Development Corporation's Ontario Book Initiative. We fur-
ther acknowledge the support of the Canada Council for the Arts and the Ontario Arts
Council for our publishing program.

Design: Terri Nimmo

Printed and bound in Canada

1 2 3 4 5 6   08 07 06 05 04 03

To my sister Wendy.

– K. S.

To a special sister, Rita Vogt,
who has been an inspiration and encouragement
throughout our lives.

– N. H. and E. H.

The author extends his appreciation
to Kathy Lowinger and the Tundra Staff.

Lost

There was once a king who was renowned for his skills as a great hunter. Early one morning, he went hunting with his men in the dark forest that surrounded his castle. He spied a stag the likes of which he had never seen before and he gave chase on his magnificent horse. His steed was able to follow quickly, but the horses of his men could not keep pace and they were soon left behind. The stag led the king into the depths of the forest until the animal completely disappeared among the trees.

The king soon realized that he was lost. He dismounted his horse and looked closely for a way out of the forest. The day passed while he wandered through the dense trees looking for a trail or path that might lead him to his men or his castle. As the sun set, he began to look for shelter; he knew it would be easier to find his way by the light of the morning sun.

The king was gazing at a large tree wondering whether he could sleep resting against its trunk when suddenly, from behind him, an old woman called out, "You there!"

Startled, the king answered, "Good Woman." He was afraid that she might be a witch, but still he called, "Good Woman, can you show me the way out of the forest?"

The old woman came closer and saw his royal robes. "Yes, Your Highness, indeed I can help you. But I have one condition. This is my enchanted forest. If you do not agree to give me what I ask, then you will never find your way out."

"What is your condition?" asked the king.

"I have a beautiful daughter, the most beautiful woman in your kingdom. If you agree to make her your wife, and the queen, then I will show you the way out."

The king did not reply. *What was he to do?*

"Let me show her to you. I know you will want her to be your queen," she said smiling.

The witch led him to her hut. Sitting by the fire was the most beautiful young woman the king had ever seen. Nevertheless he was afraid of her; he was afraid of her beauty.

"I will marry your daughter, but I too have a condition. I must prepare for the wedding. Show me out of the forest and in three days' time, I promise you that we will celebrate our wedding."

The witch looked at him closely. "I shudder to think what will happen if you break your promise," she said, with a wicked smile.

"I shall not," he replied.

The witch led him through the woods to a path that wound its way to the palace. It took only a few minutes, for indeed that part of the forest was enchanted. "In three days, my daughter will arrive at the castle. She will be the most beautiful queen your kingdom has ever seen." And with those words she disappeared.

A Ball of Golden Yarn

The king had been married once before to a good and loyal queen, but she had died some years ago. They had twelve children. There were eleven princes and one young princess, Elise. He loved his children more than anything in the world and was always concerned for their safety. Now fear gripped his heart. He worried that his new wife, the witch's daughter, might mistreat or even harm his precious children. The reason he had asked the old woman for three days was simple: he wanted to hide his children from his new wife and queen, lest she cast a spell on them.

The king sought help from a wise old woman, a woman who had been an advisor to his own mother. Together with the children, they went deep into the forest to a hidden castle. "The young princes and princess can live here without fear of the new queen," his old advisor said with a sad smile.

The old woman pulled a ball of golden yarn out of one of her deep pockets and said, "This enchanted yarn will lead you to your children. It is the only way to find them."

The King was relieved to know that only he would be able to find his daughter and sons. He kissed each child good-bye and returned to his castle with the wise old woman.

At the end of three days' time, the witch's daughter arrived. The king's castle had been made ready for the royal wedding. Flowers festooned the entrance and rose petals were scattered on the road leading to the castle. Everyone in the kingdom agreed that the bride-to-be was indeed the most beautiful woman they had ever seen. However, the king feared that she could be as wicked as she was beautiful.

After the wedding, the new queen stayed by the king and watched him closely, but still he managed to slip away each day to visit his children. Wanting to know where he disappeared to, the queen searched the castle and the grounds for him.

"Where does he go?" she asked the servants. They would not tell. She tried to bribe them with pieces of gold and silver, but still they would not tell.

Every day the queen watched the king more closely, until one day she saw him take a ball of yarn from a hiding place under his throne. She watched him as he rolled it out and then traced its path into the forest. When he returned and hid the yarn, she followed his example and let the yarn lead her. To her surprise, it led her to the hidden castle.

As the queen neared the garden outside the castle she stopped, careful not to get too close, for there playing amongst the statues were eleven young princes.

She ran back to the palace and immediately set to work. Having learned witchcraft from her mother, the wicked queen made white silk shirts for each of the princes with a magic spell sewn in.

The next day, when the king had once again gone out on a hunt, his queen took her shirts, went to the king's throne to retrieve the yarn, and followed it deep into the forest. This time she rushed right up to the castle. The princes were not used to having visitors. They thought she was their father and rushed out. The wicked queen threw a magic shirt over each one of them. The moment the shirts touched the princes, they were turned into swans. Up they flew into the air and soared away over the trees and their castle.

The queen went home delighted, thinking she was rid of her stepchildren. She did not know that the princess Elise had not run to meet her with her brothers. Elise had been working inside the castle, as she did every afternoon, preparing their evening meal. The wicked queen did not know that Elise even existed.

Into the Deep Woods

*P*oor Elise was afraid to stay in the castle alone, and in her heart she longed to find her brothers.

When dusk came, she began her journey through the trees, not knowing which direction to follow. But Elise trusted her heart. It led her deeper into the forest. She walked all night and all the next day. When night fell once again, she found a bed of soft moss and leaned her head against the trunk of a tree. All night long she dreamed of her brothers. In her dreams, they were all children again, playing with their father.

When Elise awoke the sun was high. The air was fragrant and the birds seemed to be singing just for her. She smiled, for she had slept deeply. Hearing the gurgling of water, she followed the sound and found a pool of clear water. Elise was startled when she saw her reflection on the liquid mirror.

The girl staring back at her looked quite unkempt, not at all like a princess. Elise washed her face and bathed in the water. When she emerged from the pool and braided her hair, she was once again the most beautiful girl in the kingdom.

After a breakfast of berries and water, Elise set off again to search for her brothers. Once more she let her heart lead her through the trees. The forest was so still her footsteps echoed through the trees as she walked. The foliage was thick, but somehow there was always an opening just large enough for Elise to squeeze through. There was no path, and yet Elise seemed to know what direction to walk in. As the sun grew dim, she looked for a spot where she could rest.

That night the forest was dark – so dark that not even a firefly shimmered in the air. As she lay on a bed of moss, she looked to the sky and it seemed as if an angel were smiling down at her. When she awoke, she could not tell whether or not the angel had been a dream.

Elise's journey through the forest in search of her brothers lasted many days. She was always able to find food and a place to rest. She thanked God for providing the berries, nuts, and other wild foods she found.

And so passed seven days. On the eighth day, she met an old woman who was carrying a basket of apples. She took pity on Elise and, with a smile, gave her an apple. Elise thanked her and asked if perhaps she had seen her brothers, eleven princes, in the woods.

"No," said the woman, "but a few days ago, I saw a most peculiar sight. Eleven swans swam in the river by my hut. On each swan I thought I saw a golden crown. I have never seen a swan with a crown before."

"Oh, will you take me to the river?" asked Elise.

The old woman led Elise to her hut and pointed in the direction that the swans had been swimming. "This river flows out to sea. Follow the river," she said. The old woman gave Elise another apple and wished her well on her journey. Elise thanked her and quickly ran down to the banks of the river.

Elise followed the river until she reached the great sea, where a wide expanse of water stretched ahead of her. *Where was she to go? How was she to continue?* She walked along the shore marveling at the smooth stones that had been washed up. Rolling one stone between her fingers, she spied eleven white swan feathers scattered on the rocks. She rushed to pick them up. They were wet, but Elise couldn't tell if it was from the water or from her tears.

Carrying the feathers, Elise wandered along the shore. The sun grew dim and as it was slipping beneath the horizon, eleven swans – each with a golden tuft on his head – flew toward the land. They flew one behind the other looking like a white ribbon floating through the air.

Excitement, uncertainty, and fear gripped Elise. She climbed away from the shore and hid behind some rushes. The swans, flapping their long white wings, flew down close to her. When the sun sank beneath the water, their feathers fell from their bodies. Once again, her brothers stood beside her.

She dashed out from the rushes calling each of their names and threw herself into their arms. The princes were amazed to see her. They laughed together, happy to be reunited with their sister, but soon they were discussing how wickedly their stepmother had acted.

The eldest brother explained what they had learned since becoming swans: "We can fly or swim as long as the sun is in the sky, but when it sets we appear again in our human forms. We must always find a safe resting place before sunset, for if we are flying in the clouds over the sea when the sun sets, we will take our human shape, fall into the water, and drown. We can no longer live here, so close to our father's kingdom; we must live in another land. It is more beautiful than this one, but it is far across the water. The trip across the sea takes two days and there is no island to rest on."

The youngest brother hurried to take up the story: "We fly all day to reach a rock in the middle of the sea. There we stop to change into our human forms and stand on the rock all night long. In the morning, we turn into swans once again and fly across the rest of the sea. If the weather is rough, the waves crash over us all night long and we hold onto each other so that no one is swept out to sea."

Her eldest brother continued: "We fly here looking for you, but we can stay here for only two days and then we must return to the other side of the sea. Now that we have found you, how can we take you with us? We have neither boat nor ship."

"How can I break this spell?" asked Elise. Her brothers did not have an answer but stayed up talking most of the night. At first they discussed ways to break the spell or fly across the sea, but then they laughed and remembered their happier days with the king and their mother the queen.

The next morning, the rustling of feathers awakened Elise. She opened her eyes just in time to see her brothers turn once

again into swans. The swans flew high above her, making wider and wider circles. One swan remained on the shore. It was her youngest brother who stayed by her side and rested his head in her lap. They spent the whole day together walking on the shore and watching the waves on the sea.

As the sun sank in the sky, the other swans returned, and when the sun had set, her brothers stood on the firm ground beside her.

"Our wings are strong enough to fly you over the sea! We must leave tomorrow. Have you the courage to come with us?" asked the eldest brother.

"Oh, yes, take me with you" begged Elise.

That night everyone helped gather bark and rushes, which Elise and her youngest brother wove into a mat. Once it was finished, Elise, exhausted, lay down on the mat and slept. When the sun rose and her brothers turned into swans, they gripped the mat with their beaks and flew into the air with their dear sister. She was still sleeping and, as the sun was shining full upon her face, one brother flew over her to shield her with his wings.

Across the Sea

They were far from shore when Elise awoke. It seemed so strange to be flying. Lying beside her was a pile of berries, which she knew her youngest brother had gathered for her. He was the swan flying above her, shielding her from the bright sun. As thanks she could offer him only a smile.

The swans flew all day. Carefully Elise leaned over the edge of the mat to watch the sea pass by below. They were so high in the air that a ship passing beneath them seemed like a bird floating on the water. The swans were flying much slower than they usually did, for they had the weight of their sister to bear. As the sun lowered in the sky, Elise began to worry. *Would they reach the rock in the middle of the sea in time for her brothers to regain their human form? If it took much longer, they would lose their feathers, their*

wings, and they would all drown. Elise could see that a
storm was brewing and the lowering sun proved that
evening approached. Her brothers beat their wings faster
and faster, but there was no sign of the rock. Elise knew that
it would be her fault if they did not find the rock in time.
She tried to pray but could not concentrate on anything
other than the sun on the horizon. Elise watched it sink
lower and lower and still she could not see a rock anywhere.

The sun was halfway below the water when the swans
suddenly shot downward. Elise thought that she would
surely fall off the mat, but as she gripped the edges tightly,
she saw the little rock below them. It looked like the head
of a seal popping out of the water. The sun was sinking
quickly when her foot touched the rock. In no time her
brothers stood around her, arm in arm. They hurriedly
rolled up the mat just as the storm brought the sea crashing
down all around them, with showers of foam cascading over
their heads. Flashes of lightning and claps of thunder followed each other, but the brothers and sister held on to each
other tightly. Their voices rose up in a song of prayer, giv-
ing them comfort and courage.

When morning came, the air was still, but the waves were
rough and crashed against the rock. The swans flew away

with Elise on her mat. From the height of the clouds, the white foam on the water looked like millions of swimming swans. As Elise and her brothers flew through the sky, the clouds appeared to be distant lands, each more magnificent than the last. They flew all day, until Elise saw mountains in the distance and knew that land was near. When they finally reached the shore, Elise climbed off the mat near a cavern by the water's edge.

When her brothers returned to their human form, they lead their sister into the cavern and showed her where they slept. The ground was covered with a beautiful carpet of plants. In their exhaustion, they all settled down to sleep. Elise's youngest brother asked what she hoped to dream of that night. "I only want to dream of the way to free you from the spell that holds you in its power," she replied. It was with that wish that she fell asleep.

That night, deep dreams gave Elise the answer she was searching for. When she awoke, she knew that she would have to make eleven shirts. The challenge was that the fabric had to be woven from stinging nettles that grew about the cavern, in the forest, and in graveyards. She would have to pluck the nettles, even though they would sting her hands; trample them with her feet; make yarn from them and weave it into shirts with long sleeves. When these shirts were thrown over her brothers, the spell would be broken.

But there was one condition: she must not utter a word. A single syllable from her lips would be like a dagger through her brothers' hearts. She could feel a stinging in her fingers and looked down to discover a nettle clutched in her hand. It burned like fire, and so Elise knew the truth of her dream and the task that lay ahead of her.

That morning, alone in the cavern, she began the dreary work of collecting the nettles. Her delicate hands burned as she touched them. Soon her arms were scratched and her fingers blistered, yet she bore the pain willingly. Her brothers would be free. It would take years, but her brothers

would be free. She trampled the nettles with her bare feet and then spun them into yarn.

When the sun set and her brothers returned, Elise's silence frightened them. They thought she was caught by another spell, until they saw her sore, blistered hands. Then they realized that their sister was working for their freedom. The youngest brother wept and when his tears fell on her hands, the blisters disappeared.

That night, Elise slept for only a few hours. She awoke at dawn to continue working. She could not rest until she had released her brothers. All day, and that evening too, she sat silently at her task. In a few days, she had finished one shirt. Then she began the second.

A Royal Wedding

By the time Elise had completed the fourth shirt, she had used up most of the nettles that grew near the cavern. She had to wander far from their shelter into the woods to find more.

Late one afternoon, while she was wearily returning with a great bundle of nettles, a dog burst through the bushes. Two others immediately followed and though their loud barking frightened Elise, she did not utter a sound. The dogs were followed by a group of hunters including a handsome king. The king was struck by Elise's appearance. Never had he seen a more beautiful maiden. "How came you here?" he asked.

Elise only shook her head, for she dared not speak. A single word could cost her brothers their lives.

"We won't hurt you," he reassured her. "Why do you wander all alone in these woods?"

With each question, Elise only shook her head. The king spoke many languages and asked her name in every manner he could think of. But Elise said nothing.

Her beauty had captured the king's heart, so he took off his rich cloak and placed it over her shoulders. He lifted her up and placed her gently on his horse. Though tears streamed down her face, the king rode back to his palace with Elise.

Elise cared nothing for the beautiful palace. The marble halls and richly embroidered hangings that covered the walls were meaningless to her. Female attendants brought Elise to a chamber, where she was dressed in richly adorned garments. Soft gloves covered her hands and hid the painful blisters.

That evening, when Elise entered the dining hall, her beauty was dazzling. All the courtiers bowed low before her. There had never been such a beautiful woman at the palace. Though Elise said nothing, her gentle manner and her beauty continued to captivate the king.

At the end of the meal, the king announced that he had chosen this young woman to be his wife. Music played to bring joy to the celebration, but Elise sat without even a smile on her face. It was only later in the evening, when the king led his soon-to-be bride to a little room beside her bedchamber, that she smiled. He had instructed his men to bring her weaving and all the nettles to the palace so that she would be reminded of home. "Here you may find yourself thinking of your former life," he said. Elise realized that her brothers might still be freed from the spell and, with a smile, she kissed the king's hand.

The next morning, bells rang to announce the coming marriage, but not all were joyful. One powerful duke was greatly displeased. He did not like anyone to be closer to the king than he was. He whispered to all those who would listen, "This woman is surely a witch; she has placed a spell on the king. She has no speech and yet she has our king under her power." He went to the king and suggested that the woman was not worthy to be queen, but the king paid no heed. Indeed, the next day the king and Elise were married.

Elise learned to love the king, for he adored her with all his heart and he was kind and gentle. How she longed to tell him of her brothers and the spell, but she could not. Every night she would steal away into her little room, turn the nettles into yarn, and then work on making shirts. But she had only a few hours each night in which to work, and now it was taking Elise much longer to complete her task. When she finished the seventh shirt, all of her yarn was gone and she did not have any more nettles.

To the Graveyard

The only spot where Elise could find nettles was in the little graveyard behind an old church, not too far from the palace. She was relieved that the moon was full as she slipped out of the palace, for she could make her way by its light. Though her heart was filled with dread, she knew that she must find the nettles and finish her task. She hurried down lanes and along the winding pathways leading to the churchyard. When she reached her destination, she walked all the way around the church to the graveyard. There, in the darkest corner behind the largest tombstones, grew the stinging nettles.

In the shadows Elise was sure that she could see witches sitting on the graves, but she simply hurried past them. She was determined not to stop until she had her arms filled with her stinging prize. Indeed, in no time she had gathered

the nettles. Her arms were scratched and her fingers blistered, but she quickly carried her treasure back to the palace. Only one person saw her return. It was the duke. Now he knew what he would have to do.

The next morning the duke told the king that his wife was a witch and that she had joined all the other witches in the graveyard the night before. The king did not believe him, so the duke went to the king's mother and told her all that he believed. He said that the young queen, who had come from who knows where, had enchanted the king. "The king has been placed under a spell, and that is why he married her."

The king's mother loved her son dearly and she agreed to keep watch on the new queen. Each night she hid behind a tapestry to spy on Elise as she went to the little room, trampled the nettles with her bare feet, wound the fibers into yarn, and then sat for hours weaving shirts. The king's mother was distressed, for she did not understand the young queen's strange activity. She told the king of her fears.

"Your queen has taken trips to the graveyard, where she meets with witches. Every night she sits and weaves shirts – what are they for? It is surely to send you and your court under a spell." The king did not believe her at first, but then at night he too began to watch Elise slip out of bed and into the little room where she feverishly worked on her shirts.

His face grew darker each day. Elise worried, but she worried more about her brothers. When she finished the shirts she would be able to break the spell that bound her brothers and reveal her secret to her beloved husband. Only one shirt remained to weave, but Elise had no more nettles. She would have to go to the graveyard one last time.

She shuddered at the thought of the trip – of the graves and of the witches – but when she thought of her brothers, she knew that she had to go that very night. When Elise slipped through a little-used doorway at the rear of the palace, she didn't know that the king, his mother, and the duke were following her. She hurried along the dark lanes and pathways until she finally reached the graveyard. When the king saw her enter with the witches sitting on the graves, he was shocked and hurt. He thought then that the duke was right. His wife was a witch. "Let the people judge her," was all he could say as he ran back to the palace.

Unaware that the king had seen her, Elise ran quickly to gather the nettles. When she returned to the palace, the duke

was waiting at the doorway. "You will sleep in the prison tonight," he said, with a menacing laugh. "Those nettles can be your bed."

Elise could say nothing as she was led down to the prison. She was left alone in her dank, dark cell. The door opened only once. The king's mother brought the ten shirts. "You can use these as your pillow and your blankets," she said with disgust.

Elise simply got to work. She had only one shirt left to make. All night she trampled the nettles, wound the yarn, and toward daybreak started weaving the last shirt.

The king had said that the people would judge her, and indeed they did. They found her guilty of being a witch and, like all witches, she was to be burnt at the stake. Elise heard people outside her window telling of the sentence, but that only made her work harder. Her judgment was to be carried out the next day. The king was brokenhearted, but he could not face seeing his wife again.

When the sun was setting, Elise heard the rustling of wings outside her window. She continued to work on the final shirt, but when she heard her youngest brother call to her, she knew that her brothers had finally found her. She could not reply. Instead she simply worked her fingers, raw with blisters and sores, as quickly as she could.

During the night, eleven young men pounded on the door of the palace demanding to see the king, but they were told that he could not be wakened. They begged, they prayed, they even threatened, but it was only when the sun began to rise that the king made his way to the palace gate. The men were gone. There were only swans, eleven of them, flying over the palace.

That day, Elise kept busy working on the last shirt, while outside the palace they were preparing for the great fire that would end her life. People came from all over the kingdom and the surrounding countryside for the event. It was not often there was this much excitement. Though the king hated the thought of the spectacle, he knew that he would have to attend.

Elise was led from the prison to the stake that had been erected in front of the palace. She carried the shirts over her arm as she tried to finish the left sleeve of the last one.

She was led up to the stake, but before anyone could light the fire, eleven swans flew through the sky and landed at her feet. Her heart filled with joy! She had been waiting so long for this moment. Quickly she threw the shirts over each of them. As soon as the shirts touched their bodies, their feathers fell from them and each young man stood strong and handsome. Only the youngest lacked his left arm – in its place was a swan's wing.

The eleven brothers hugged and kissed Elise. Elise was near faint from exhaustion and joy, but she went to the king. "Dearest husband, I was falsely accused." Elise told him of her task and how she had been unable to speak. In a rage, the king quickly banished the duke from the kingdom. The king's mother dropped to her knees and begged forgiveness of the young queen. Elise helped the old woman back to her feet and assured her of her love. Tears of joy streamed down the face of the king. Church bells rang, though no one was in the church. All the wood that had been gathered for the fire turned into a giant rosebush and burst forth into bloom. The king plucked a large white rose from the bush and gave it to Elise. The sky filled with doves, the crowd of people cheered, and arm in arm the king led Elise – his wife and queen – and her brothers back into the palace. Together they lived in happiness and peace for many years.

The Art of
Paper Cutting

*P*aper cutting had been practiced in China for centuries by the time it made its way to Europe in the 1600s. Paper cutting requires paper, and paper was, at the time, a hand-made treasure. It was available mostly to the very rich or to the Church.

Monks used it for gorgeous manuscripts, decorating the texts with glowing miniature paintings and exquisite paper cut designs.

Paper stencils based on Asian and African designs were lacquered or oiled so they wouldn't absorb paint and were used to decorate the walls of churches. Religious paper cuts called prayer papers were a cherished item to give and receive on holy days in northern Germany.

After the invention of the printing press, paper ceased to be a rare luxury and pattern books full of stencil designs became available. Many of the patterns that antique lovers appreciate today in furniture, embroidery, and in art can be traced back to those paper cut stencils.

By the seventeenth century, paper cutting, or *scherenschnitt*, had become a popular kind of folk art in Germany and Switzerland, where various ways of cutting paper evolved. Some cutouts were made from single-folded papers. Others were cut from flat sheets. Color wasn't the focus – most *scherenschnitte* were cut from black or white paper – it was the delicacy and design of the shapes that engaged the artist.

People continued to find ways to use *scherenschnitte*. Professional scribes decorated legal documents with cut work, glued them to fabric or good paper, and then rolled or folded them up for safekeeping, using shapes from the original cutting to seal them. The documents were not only beautiful, but also hard to forge.

Paper cut greeting cards and bookmarks were so popular that when people left Germany and Switzerland for North America, the cards crossed the ocean with them. We enjoy them as valentines to this day.

Paper cutting was also an important art form in Jewish culture. Often it was men or boys who worked on single-folded paper. Pictures and documents like marriage contracts were decorated with symbols drawn from the Bible.

Portuguese Jewish immigrants brought the art with them when they fled to Holland in the early seventeenth century, and it quickly became popular all over the country. The Dutch adapted the art by using knives as well as scissors to make paper carvings called *schneiden*.

Soon paper cutting was a familiar art form and the pictures included all kinds of designs and figures, not just religious themes. Colored *Scherenschnitte* illustrated German fairy tales. The Danish storyteller Hans Christian Andersen also practiced the art.

Possibly the best-known kind of paper cutting is the silhouette. Silhouettes were named after Étienne de Silhouette, the vastly unpopular controller general of finances in France during the time of Louise XV. He was such a miser that his name was used for anything that was cheap. In the days before photography, when a painted portrait was a luxury, paper profiles were a way to preserve the image of loved ones. Some were tiny to fit into a locket, and others were as big as their subjects, but all of them were a source of pleasure to people across Europe.

Silhouette artists traveled from village to village, the forerunners of today's professional photographers who capture our images as important family keepsakes.

Silhouettes have given way to photography, but the art of paper cutting continues to delight. Nelly and Ernst Hofer learned their art in their native Switzerland and have passed it on to their children, Ben and Jasmin. *Scherenschnitt's* delicacy and magic is the perfect way to make fairy tales come to life.